The Great Adventure of
WO TI

Nathan Zimelman ◆ *Illustrated by* Julie Downing

Macmillan Publishing Company *New York*
Maxwell Macmillan Canada *Toronto*
Maxwell Macmillan International *New York Oxford Singapore Sydney*

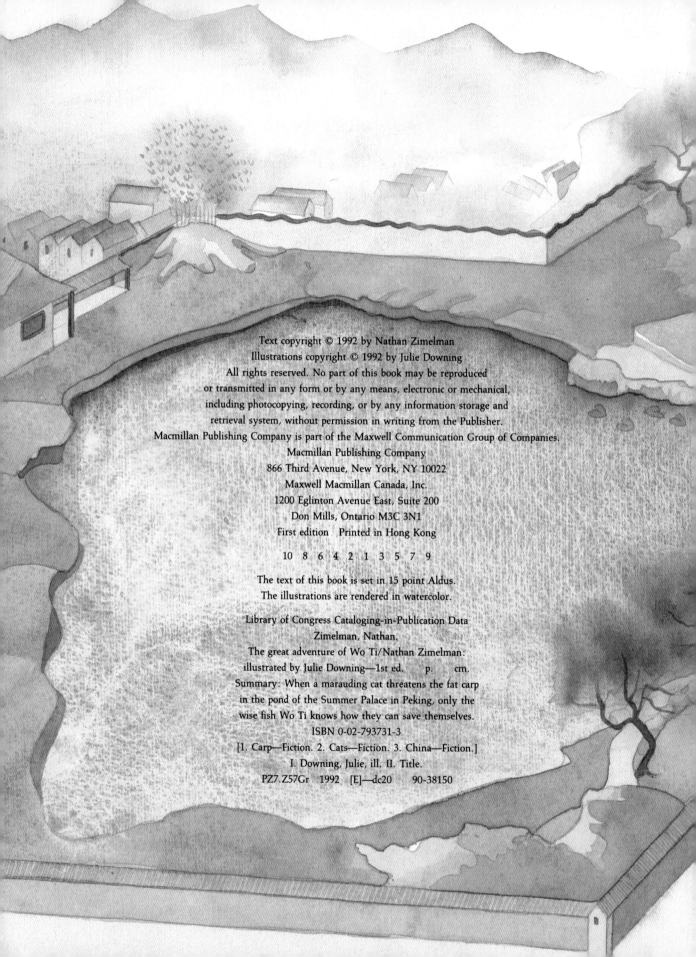

Macmillan Publishing Company is part of the Maxwell Communication Group of Companies.
Macmillan Publishing Company
866 Third Avenue, New York, NY 10022
Maxwell Macmillan Canada, Inc.
1200 Eglinton Avenue East, Suite 200
Don Mills, Ontario M3C 3N1
First edition   Printed in Hong Kong

10 8 6 4 2 1 3 5 7 9

The text of this book is set in 15 point Aldus.
The illustrations are rendered in watercolor.

Library of Congress Cataloging-in-Publication Data
Zimelman, Nathan.
The great adventure of Wo Ti/Nathan Zimelman:
illustrated by Julie Downing—1st ed.   p.   cm.
Summary: When a marauding cat threatens the fat carp
in the pond of the Summer Palace in Peking, only the
wise fish Wo Ti knows how they can save themselves.
ISBN 0-02-793731-3
[1. Carp—Fiction. 2. Cats—Fiction. 3. China—Fiction.]
I. Downing, Julie, ill. II. Title.
PZ7.Z57Gr 1992 [E]—dc20   90-38150

For Sarah Zimelman
—N. Z.
To Michael and Angela
—J. D.

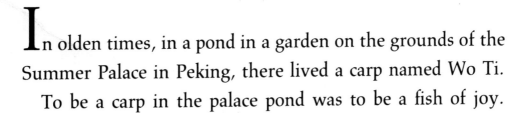

In olden times, in a pond in a garden on the grounds of the Summer Palace in Peking, there lived a carp named Wo Ti.

To be a carp in the palace pond was to be a fish of joy.

Here no fisherman dangled his line, seeking to make the carp his evening meal.

Here was never a danger that the water would be drunk dry by the summer sun.

Here the animals and birds were so well fed that when they came to the pond, they came only to look.

There was of course much hunger outside the garden's walls. But the walls were so high that hunger had not been able to climb over.

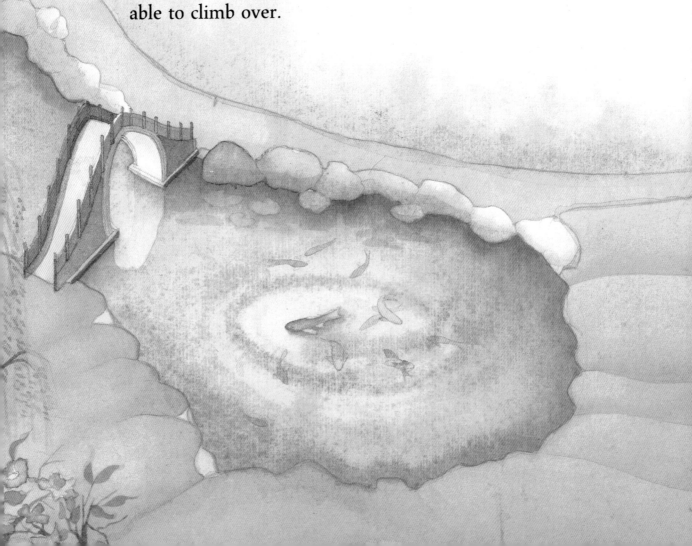

The carp themselves never wanted. The many bushes and flowers provided an easy harvest of insects. And the children who lived in the palace were always bringing tidbits from the palace tables to feed their favorite fish.

It was a fine life the carp led. They swam slowly in the gentle warmth of the water, while their small cousins, the goldfish, flitted in and out, their rainbow colors a pleasantness to behold. There was food enough and time enough to grow old and fat and lazy.

Yet one carp was not contented, and that was Wo Ti. What it was that he missed in his life he did not know. But while the other carp lazed through each day, Wo Ti would swim impatiently from one end of the pond to the other, searching. He looked and looked until the other carp would flick their tails and cry, "Let us be, Wo Ti! Let us be!"

And then Kitti Ho appeared in the garden.

A pack of shrieking boys and yapping dogs had discovered the cat prowling the alleys of Peking. As is the way of boys and dogs, with one mind and one voice they began to chase the cat.

Smiling a cat smile, Kitti Ho ran.

But although he was the cleverest of cats, he could not get away. Wherever Kitti Ho ran, up alley and down, there were the boys and the dogs.

At last, before Kitti Ho there rose the high and unending walls of the garden of the Summer Palace, the supposedly unclimbable walls of the Summer Palace.

With all his might, Kitti Ho leaped. Scratching and scrambling, up and up he went until he stood upon the top of the walls that all said could never be climbed.

Below him the boys shouted and the dogs howled.

Before him lay paradise.

He turned and smiled a cat smile on loud and busy Peking. Then he clambered down the other side of the wall, and, a streak of gray, Kitti Ho entered the grounds of the Summer Palace.

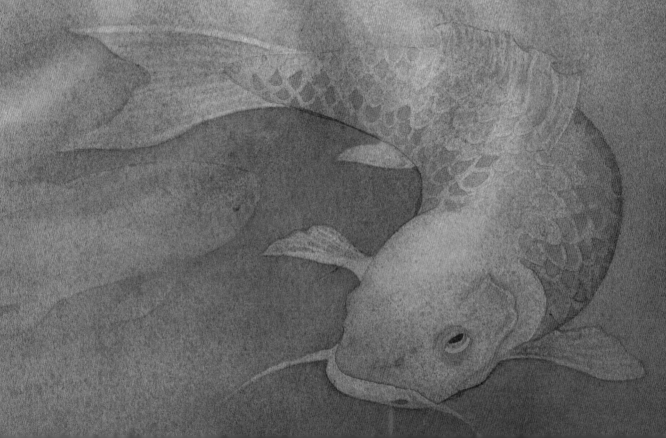

A cat that can survive in the back alleys of Peking can live well indeed in such a place as Kitti Ho now found himself.

The birds perched fat and unknowing in the trees.

The shallows of the pond were rich with foolish little goldfish.

In the beginning Kitti Ho did his hunting at night, when he knew that humans would not be about.

Each morning would find one bird fewer, one small goldfish gone from the pond. But there were so many of both that neither the gardeners nor the children could tell.

When the gardeners and the children were about, Kitti Ho lay hidden and asleep.

Time passed, and Kitti Ho grew bolder. He began to hunt in the day, as if he and not the emperor were the owner of the palace grounds.

After he had done his hunting, Kitti Ho liked to crouch by the side of Wo Ti's pond. Edging out as far as he could on the rocks that reached toward the center of the water, he would bat at the fish with his paw.

He had not yet caught more than goldfish doing this. Still, even at the full of the sun, the water no longer felt warm to the carp, for Kitti Ho had brought cold fear to their pond.

One afternoon, the shivering carp were gathered in the middle of the pond. They were no longer fat and lazy, but thin and given to short jumps when even a bee's shadow passed over the water.

Each cried to the other, "What shall be done?"

It was then that Wo Ti spoke his wonderful idea. "We shall become rocks," he said.

The other fish swam around Wo Ti. "How can we be rocks when we are fish? And if we are rocks, what will that do?"

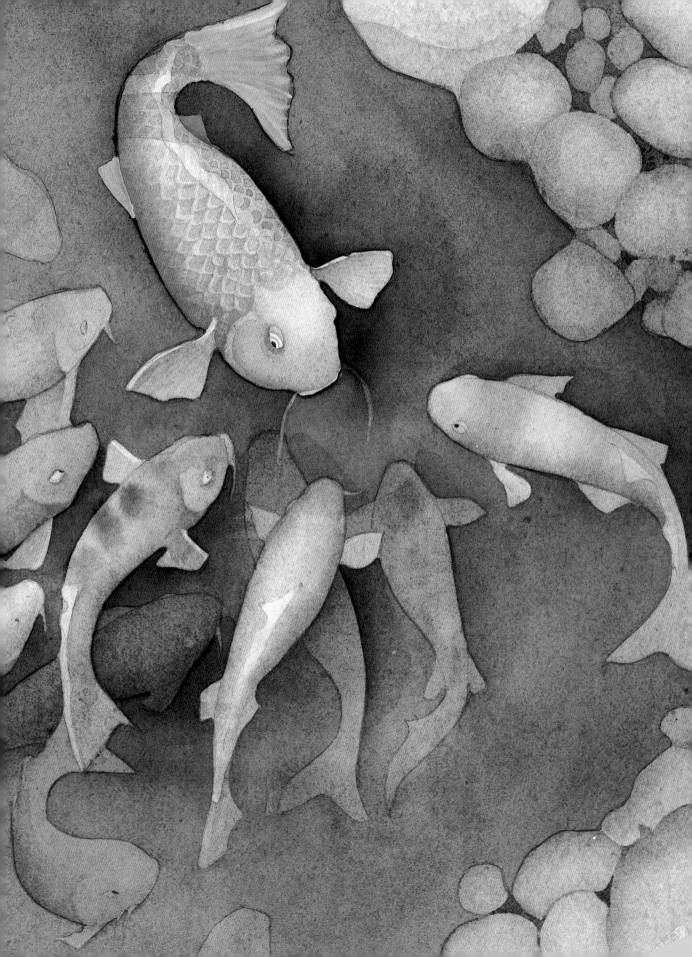

"If we pretend we are rocks," said Wo Ti, "then the cat will be able to walk to the center of the pond. He will walk on our backs to the center of the pond."

"He will catch us then!" cried the other fish. "He will eat us then!"

"No." Wo Ti dove deep and, rising, spoke again. "When he has come to the center of the pool, we will turn back into the fish that we are. He will fall into the water."

"Into our water!"

Wo Ti swam rapidly around the pond. "Water, water, water, and we are fish, and he is a cat."

The other carp shuddered. "He is a cat."

The next afternoon, when Kitti Ho came to watch at the edge of the pond, he saw what seemed to be a path of rocks reaching to the very center of the pond, where Wo Ti was splashing splendidly.

Kitti Ho was wise in the ways of the streets. There he would have peered at even the smallest change from all sides before venturing a single one of his lives.

Here, on the grounds of the Summer Palace, only humans were to be feared. All else, even rocks appearing where rocks had never been before, was as it should be to Kitti Ho.

Without any thought in his head but a taste of carp, Kitti Ho ran across the backs of the fish.

When he was at the center of the pond, the carp dove to the bottom. Kitti Ho floundered and yowled and beat the water to a froth.

Out of the west and north and south and east the palace gardeners erupted.

And, in not too long a time, a bedraggled Kitti Ho found himself tossed back into the streets of Peking.

At the Summer Palace, life was much as it had been before Kitti Ho and fear had appeared.

The birds perched, contented, on the tree branches.

The insects sang their sleepy songs over the flowers.

Only in the carp pond was all not as it had been. The carp grew fat and lazily contented, but the fattest and most lazily contented was Wo Ti. It was apparent that he no longer felt that anything was missing in his life.

Maybe it was because he had had his great adventure.